SOMETHING'S FISHY

SOMETHING'S FISHY

Jeff Szpirglas AND **Danielle Saint-Onge**
ILLUSTRATIONS BY **Dave Whamond**

ORCA BOOK PUBLISHERS

Library and Archives Canada Cataloguing in Publication

Szpirglas, Jeff
Something's fishy / Jeff Szpirglas and Danielle Saint-Onge ;
illustrated by Dave Whamond.
(Orca echoes)

Issued also in electronic format.
ISBN 978-1-55469-787-8

I. Saint-Onge, Danielle II. Whamond, Dave
III. Title. IV. Series: Orca echoes
PS8637.Z65S64 2011   JC813'.6   C2010-907916-7

First published in the United States, 2011
Library of Congress Control Number: 2010941958

Summary: A rambunctious boy swallows the class pet
and has to find a way to make it up to his classmates.

Orca Book Publishers gratefully acknowledges the support for its publishing programs
provided by the following agencies: the Government of Canada through the Canada Book Fund
and the Canada Council for the Arts, and the Province of British Columbia
through the BC Arts Council and the Book Publishing Tax Credit.

MIX
Paper from
responsible sources
FSC® C011825

*Orca Book Publishers is dedicated to preserving the environment and has printed this book
on paper certified by the Forest Stewardship Council.®*

Typesetting by Jasmine Devonshire
Cover artwork and interior illustrations by Dave Whamond
Author photo by Tim Basile

ORCA BOOK PUBLISHERS   ORCA BOOK PUBLISHERS
PO Box 5626, STN. B   PO Box 468
VICTORIA, BC CANADA   CUSTER, WA USA
V8R 6S4   98240-0468

www.orcabook.com
Printed and bound in Canada.

14 13 12 11 • 4 3 2 1

To our students,
who inspire fiction daily.

Chapter One

The end of the school day had arrived. Mr. Claxton's grade-two class sat in a circle on the carpet. They were excited. Mr. Claxton had promised them a surprise.

Kamal raised his hand. "Is the surprise that we don't have to write a math quiz tomorrow?"

Mr. Claxton smiled. "No, there's still a math quiz."

Eva raised her hand. "Is it an extra-long recess?"

Mr. Claxton shook his head.

"I know! I know!" Miles said. "We are going to have a dance party!"

Mr. Claxton shook his head again.

"It's extra recess AND a dance party," said Kamal.

Mr. Claxton smiled. "Nice try. The surprise is a class pet."

Twenty-one sets of eyes opened wide. Twenty-one mouths dropped open. Mr. Claxton's students gasped so loudly, they could be heard next door.

"A pet! Woo-hoo!" said Kamal. "Is it a dog?"

Mr. Claxton turned his rain stick over. The beads tinkled softly down the inside. He leaned back in his chair and waited for the class to quiet down. "I haven't decided what kind of pet we're going to have. Maybe you have some ideas for me," said Mr. Claxton.

"A dog! A dog!" shouted Kamal. He had never had a dog before, and he really wanted one.

"Let's get a teddy-bear hamster." Eva giggled. "They're so cute!"

"How about a guinea pig?" Miles asked.

At the back of the room, a hand went up. The class groaned. "Oh, great," Miles said.

Jamie sat at the back, near the class library. He liked to flip through nature books about wild animals during circle time. Mr. Claxton took a deep breath. "Yes, Jamie?"

Jamie was so excited, he jumped to his feet. He kept jumping. "I think we should get—"

"A shark?" Kamal asked.

Jamie's eyes widened. "How did you know?"

"Because that's all you *ever* talk about. Sharks *this*. Sharks *that*," said Kamal. "Don't you think about anything else?"

Jamie shrugged. "I don't want our class to get just any shark," he said. "I think we should get a great white shark." He held his hands as far apart as he could. "It's the fiercest fish in the sea!"

Jamie loved sharks. He owned three T-shirts with sharks on them. He slept in shark pajamas. He always checked shark books out of the library. Last summer his parents took him on a road trip to the ocean. Jamie found a shark's tooth on the beach.

He had brought it to school for show-and-tell four times already.

Most of the kids in his class were tired of hearing about sharks. Jamie's parents were too. But when Jamie got excited about something, he could not stop. He didn't mean to bother people. He just thought sharks were *so* cool.

He even started his own Shark Club. It was free to join, but Jamie was the only member.

Mr. Claxton scratched his head. He always did that when he was thinking. "I don't believe there's enough space in here for a great white shark."

Jamie looked around the room. He looked at the library. He looked at the desks. He looked at his classmates. "We could move the girls to another room," he said.

"We're not getting a great white shark," said Mr. Claxton.

Jamie lowered his head, but only for a moment. "What about a tiger shark? Or a bull shark? They're good too."

"Enough with your sharks," Kamal said.

"Does that mean you don't want to join my Shark Club?" Jamie asked.

Up at the front of the class, Eva rolled her eyes. "Jamie is *so* weird," she whispered to her friend. "He can't think about anything but sharks. In gym, all he does is circle and chase us. He thinks he is a shark and we are little fish."

Once again, Mr. Claxton looked at Jamie and scratched his head. Then he smiled. "Class, I've decided on our pet. It will be here tomorrow morning."

The school bell rang. The class scrambled to leave. Everyone was excited to find out what the new pet might be.

"I bet it's a hamster," Miles said. "Eva always gets what she wants."

"No way," Kamal said. "A dog. It's totally going to be a dog."

Jamie hung back. He tiptoed up to Mr. Claxton's desk. "You know, Mr. Claxton, some sharks are really small. A spined pygmy shark is smaller than a ruler. And they don't eat people. Not even girls."

Mr. Claxton smiled. "I know, Jamie. And I think you'll really enjoy our pet when you meet it tomorrow."

Jamie could not believe what he was hearing. Was Mr. Claxton going to get a spined pygmy shark?

As he walked home, Jamie wondered if the shark would have razor-sharp teeth. Would it swim super-fast? How big of a tank would it need?

Chapter Two

Jamie had never owned a pet. He had asked his parents for a shark. "Maybe you can get a goldfish," Jamie's dad had said. "For your birthday." But Jamie's birthday was a month away.

"I think Mr. Claxton is going to bring in a pet shark," Jamie told his parents at breakfast the next day. "I can feel it!" He shoveled cereal into his mouth so fast, most of it fell onto the table.

"A shark? Are you sure?" Jamie's mom said. "Isn't that a little big for your classroom?"

Jamie shrugged. "That's why I said we should get a spined pygmy shark."

Jamie's mom knew all about spined pygmy sharks. She knew a lot about all kinds of sharks. She had bought Jamie many shark books and DVDs.

Jamie's mom also knew about the math test that day. She had helped Jamie study the night before. They practiced adding and subtracting. Jamie liked math. His favorite part was doing the greater-than and less-than signs. He knew the open end liked to "eat" the bigger number. He always drew his greater-than and less-than signs with shark teeth.

After breakfast, Jamie put on his shark baseball cap and ran to school. He was halfway down the block when his mom called him back. "Jamie, you forgot to put your shoes on!"

Jamie looked at his feet. "Oh," he said. "Oops."

"Jamie, you have got to be more responsible," she said.

"I will. I *will*!"

When he arrived at school, Jamie started chasing Eva and her friends. "I will eat you up. You are the prey, and I am the predator!" he said.

"No," Eva said. "You are Jamie, and you're just plain weird!"

Jamie shrugged and continued chasing the girls around the schoolyard.

As soon as the bell rang, Mr. Claxton's class ran to line up at the front of the school. Jamie shuffled his feet. What was the pet going to be? Would they be able to play with it?

Once they were inside, Jamie ran down the hall to his classroom. He bumped into Eva in the cloakroom.

"Hey, watch where you're going," Eva said.

"Sorry," Jamie said. He hurried to take off his coat.

"Jamie, you hung your coat on my head!" Eva shouted.

But Jamie was already in the classroom. He dove across the carpet, knocking Miles and Kamal over.

Chapter Three

Sitting on top of Mr. Claxton's bookcase was a tank covered with a cloth. Jamie went over to touch the cloth, but Mr. Claxton stepped in front of him. "I know you're excited. You have to wait until everyone else is ready."

Mr. Claxton asked Jamie to sit beside him for morning circle time. Jamie rocked back and forth. What was behind the cloth? Was it a shark? Maybe a small one?

When Jamie felt he couldn't wait any longer, Mr. Claxton pulled away the cloth. Everyone stood up. They stretched their necks and stood on their tiptoes to get a better look at the tank.

Inside the tank was a fish. It was blue and purple. It had long fins, but it hardly moved.

"It's a fish," said Eva.

"It looks dead," Kamal said.

"Why couldn't we get more than one?" Miles asked.

Mr. Claxton turned his rain stick over to quiet the class. Before he could answer, Jamie marched toward the tank. He smiled from ear to ear.

"This is a betta fish," Jamie said. He jabbed his finger at the tank. "It's a male betta fish. There's only one because if you put another male in there, they would fight."

Miles and Kamal looked at each other. "Cool!"

"The next question," Mr. Claxton said, "is what to name our fish."

Everyone had different ideas for a name. There were too many names for the class to vote on. Mr. Claxton asked everyone to sit down and write their choice on a slip of paper. Jamie knew exactly what to call the fish. He wrote the name on his paper and put it into Mr. Claxton's hat.

Once all of the papers were in the hat, Mr. Claxton reached in to pick the winner. "The person who names the fish will take care of it this week," Mr. Claxton said. He swished his hand around in the hat. "That person will need to be very responsible."

Jamie watched Mr. Claxton and hoped he would choose his name from the hat.

"Our fish will need the water in its tank changed at the end of each week," said Mr. Claxton. "Remember, we should feed it only a pinch of food a day. Too much food and the fish could get sick."

Mr. Claxton pulled out a slip of paper. "And the name of our new class pet is…" Everyone leaned forward. "Jaws!"

"Huh?" said Eva.

"What kind of name is that?" asked Kamal.

There was only one person who didn't look confused. Jamie jumped to his feet. "Jaws is the world's scariest shark!"

"Oh no." Eva gulped. "Jamie's name got picked. That means *he* is in charge of the fish this week."

"He'll probably kill it," Miles said.

Mr. Claxton got to his feet. "Watch what you're saying," he reminded the class. "Jamie is going to take extra-special care of Jaws. It's a big responsibility, but I know he will do a good job. Right, Jamie?"

Jamie stood by the fish tank, watching the betta. "Huh?" He looked up. Mr. Claxton and the rest of the class were staring at him.

"He's not even listening," Eva said.

"Sure, I'm listening." Jamie smiled. "What were you talking about?"

Chapter Four

Jamie ate his lunch beside the fish tank and watched the betta. He imagined it was a great white shark on the hunt for prey. Then he imagined himself in the ocean with the shark. He was swimming alongside the scariest fish in the sea.

Jamie looked at his lunch. He imagined his tuna sandwich was a bluefin tuna. Jamie chomped down on it. He shook his head from side to side. His teeth were sharp like a shark's. He could tear a big meaty chunk out of a fish.

Jamie shook his head so hard, bits of tuna flew across the room. The tuna splattered all over Eva's desk. "Gross!" she screamed.

Eva was good at screaming. She screamed for the lunch monitor.

The lunch monitor saw Jamie, his sandwich and the tuna on Eva's desk. The lunch monitor did not like coming to Mr. Claxton's class. She thought his class was messy, especially Jamie. She folded her arms across her chest. "Jamie, are you eating like a shark again?"

Everyone turned toward Jamie. "It wasn't me," he said and pointed at the fish tank. "It was our class shark."

The lunch monitor pointed toward the sink. "Whoever is in charge of the class pet cleans up after it."

"Okay," Jamie said.

He got up from his desk and went to the sink. He wet a brown paper towel.

"Make sure you clean it *all* up," Eva said.

Jamie looked at the clock. "There's only two minutes until recess."

Eva shrugged.

Jamie made a sour face. Eva was always trying to get him in trouble.

Jamie tried to be nice to Eva. But when he had invited her to join his Shark Club, Eva told him he was weird. Jamie didn't think he was weird. Some of the dolls Eva had brought in for show-and-tell were weird. One had scary eyes that blinked whenever its head moved. Another made baby noises when you moved its arms. Jamie thought dolls were scarier than sharks.

Jamie looked at the clock again. Time was running out. He hadn't eaten his blue Jell-O yet. How was he going to clean Eva's desk and eat dessert in time for recess?

Jamie wiped up the tuna, but he only made a bigger mess. He ran back to the sink, wet the paper towel again and finished up.

When the bell rang, Jamie groaned. There was no time for Jell-O.

Everyone rushed out of the classroom. Kamal hung back for a second. "We're playing soccer, Jamie. Can you be on defense?"

Kamal had never asked Jamie to play soccer before.

Jamie nodded. "Sure!"

He took a quick look at Eva's desk. It was clean enough.

Jamie looked around the classroom. Was there something else he was supposed to do besides eat his Jell-O?

"Come on!" Kamal shouted from the hall.

"Right. I am on defense!" Jamie said and ran outside.

Chapter Five

Max usually played defense, but he was at home sick today. So Jamie filled in for him.

Jamie usually walked around the school grounds at recess. He liked to explore. Sometimes he would look at ants. Sometimes he would think about sharks. Sometimes he would do both.

Kamal and Miles set their backpacks up as the goalposts. Everyone got into position. Jamie stood a few feet away from the goalie, Kamal. It was very hard to score on Kamal.

The other team rushed toward Jamie and Kamal with the ball.

Jamie imagined the other team was a school of tiger sharks. He imagined the ball was a tasty seal, and he was a great white shark. There was no way he was going to let the tiger sharks eat the seal.

Jamie pounced on the ball. He grabbed hold of it with his arms. He squeezed it hard.

The other players stopped.

"What are you doing?" Kamal asked. "You're supposed to be on defense."

"I invented a new game," Jamie said. "It's a type of shark soccer. I call it Sharker!"

"Sharker?" Miles asked. "What's that?"

"It's like regular soccer. Except you pretend you are a great white shark. And the ball is a seal you are trying to eat." He looked around. The other players were shaking their heads.

"I knew it was a bad idea to ask Jamie to play," said one of the boys. "He always does this."

Jamie looked at Kamal.

"We are just playing regular soccer," Kamal said.

Jamie nodded. He had to stay focused on the game. He got back into position. He was not going to think about sharks. He was going to keep his eye on the ball.

The other team ran forward. Jamie kept his eye on the ball. He was going to think about soccer. Not sharks.

Someone kicked the ball toward their net. Jamie pretended his foot was a giant shark fin and swatted the ball away.

"Nice save, Jaws," Kamal said.

Jaws! Jamie gulped. "Oh no!" he said. He ran toward the school.

"Where are you going?" Kamal said.

Jamie kept running. "Not now, Kamal. This is important!"

Kamal didn't see the other team kick the ball at his net, and they scored. Nobody ever scored on Kamal!

"Jamie, come back! We need you," Kamal said.

But Jamie was too far away to hear him. He sprinted across the school grounds. He had to get inside. The fish! He had forgotten to feed Jaws!

Jamie ran down the hall as fast as he could.

Chapter Six

Jamie burst into Mr. Claxton's classroom. He slid across the carpet. He came to a stop beside the fish tank. All the soccer and running had made him tired.

Jamie pressed his face against the tank.

The betta fish swam around.

Jamie let out a long sigh. He had never been responsible for a pet before. He had almost forgotten the most important part—feeding it! If he couldn't even remember to feed Jaws, his mom would never let him have a pet.

"Where is the fish food?" Jamie said to himself. He spun around. It wasn't on the tank's table.

He didn't see it on anyone's desk. Maybe Mr. Claxton had put it *inside* a desk.

Jamie dumped the closest desk over. Books and pencil crayons spilled to the floor. Jamie groaned. It was Eva's desk. She was not going to be happy, and there was no time to clean up.

Jamie looked at the clock above the door. There were only a few minutes of recess left. He bolted over to Mr. Claxton's desk.

There was a white plastic bottle on top that said *FISH FOOD*.

"Yes!" said Jamie. He grabbed the bottle and dashed back to the tank. He popped off the bottle's lid. It was full of little orange and brown flakes. How much was he supposed to give Jaws?

Jamie could not remember. Maybe it says how much to use on the bottom of the bottle, thought Jamie. He turned the container over.

Splash! All the fish food fell into the tank.

"Oh no!" Jamie shouted. He watched the flakes cloud the water. It was hard to see Jaws.

Then Jamie remembered what Mr. Claxton had said: *Feed it only a pinch of food a day. Too much food and the fish could get sick.*

Jaws was already eating the fish food. How was he going to keep Jaws from eating *all* the food?

Jamie reached into the tank to grab the flakes. Most of them had turned to mush. He found a small net on Mr. Claxton's desk and tried to scoop some out. But the water only got cloudier.

Jamie froze. He was much bigger than Jaws. He would eat all the fish food before Jaws had a chance.

He plunked his face into the tank. He opened his mouth and took a few bites. The fish food tasted gross. But he had a job to do. He was going to be responsible. He would eat all the food himself.

The bell rang. Jamie dunked his head underwater to try and reach the food at the bottom of the tank.

Something swished into his mouth. It tickled his throat. It was not fish food. It was not his tuna sandwich. Jaws was caught in his throat!

Jamie pulled his head out. Water splashed everywhere. He opened his mouth and coughed and coughed. But Jaws was stuck.

Jamie tried to take a deep breath, and that's when he felt Jaws slip down his throat.

He had *eaten* Jaws!

Chapter Seven

Jamie didn't know what to do. He had never eaten a fish before. At least, not a live one. He ran outside and lined up with his class.

He was nervous. The class was going to blame him. Mr. Claxton was going to get angry and call Jamie's parents. When Jamie's parents learned he had eaten Jaws, they would never let him have a pet.

Jamie felt tears in his eyes, but he wiped them away. He was going to pretend nothing had happened. If Mr. Claxton asked, Jamie planned to say Jaws jumped out of the tank. Fish could jump.

Jamie's tummy felt funny as he walked inside with his class. Behind him Kamal asked, "Jamie, are you okay?"

"Sure, sure," Jamie said. He took three deep breaths to calm himself.

"You left in the middle of the game," Kamal said. "You were doing good on defense."

"Oh," Jamie said. Nobody had ever told him he was good at soccer.

"Want to play again tomorrow?" Kamal asked.

"Sure," Jamie said. It was hard to feel good about being asked to play soccer again when he was worried about getting in trouble.

"Hey, Jamie," Kamal asked, "why is your hair all wet?"

Jamie felt his hair. It was soaked. So was the top of his T-shirt. He shrugged. "Didn't it rain?"

Kamal shook his head. "No." He narrowed his eyes. Something was up with Jamie. Something fishy.

Mr. Claxton arrived with the attendance folder. He opened the classroom door and followed the class inside.

Eva screamed.

Kamal looked at Jamie. Jamie looked at Kamal.

Eva pointed at her desk. "Someone dumped my desk on the floor." She started to pick up her stuff, and then she screamed again.

"What's wrong?" asked Mr. Claxton.

Eva bent down and picked up a drawing. "My drawing of Jaws is wet. It's ruined!" She started to cry.

At the back of the room, Jamie gulped. His face was hot. His tummy still felt funny.

Mr. Claxton looked at the picture. "How did it get so wet?"

"Look, Mr. Claxton." Eva pointed. "Look at the fish tank!"

Mr. Claxton looked. The whole class looked, and everyone gasped.

"Where's Jaws?" asked Eva.

Mr. Claxton turned to the class. "Everyone on the carpet. Now." Mr. Claxton didn't yell, but Jamie could tell he was upset.

Jamie felt terrible. Mr. Claxton was his favorite teacher.

Last year, Mrs. Ross always got frustrated when Jamie couldn't sit still. Mr. Claxton let Jamie wiggle. He knew Jamie liked to move around like a shark. Sharks never stopped moving in the water.

The class sat in a circle. Jamie tried his best not to wiggle. Mr. Claxton had never been this upset.

"Jaws is missing," Mr. Claxton said. "And there is water on the floor."

Miles put up his hand. "Maybe he jumped out of the tank."

Jamie nodded. That's what he was going to say.

Mr. Claxton shook his head. "A betta can't jump like that." Mr. Claxton looked at his students. The room was silent. Jamie's face went red, and he lowered his head.

"If any of you know who did this," Mr. Claxton said, "please come and see me at the end of the day."

Mr. Claxton looked at his students. "Now, it's time for the math test."

There were some groans from the classroom, but everyone got to their feet and went to their desks.

Jamie was the last off the carpet. Mr. Claxton was upset, and it was all his fault.

Chapter Eight

Jamie couldn't think clearly during the math test. He was dizzy. His tummy was tight. He sat in his desk and held his pencil. He kept glancing at the empty tank and rubbing his tummy. He felt sick. Would Jaws come out in his throw-up?

He didn't even do the greater-than and less-than questions or put teeth on the signs.

Jamie looked up to see Mr. Claxton standing above him. Jamie's heart raced.

"Is everything all right?" Mr. Claxton asked.

"Sure," Jamie said. Jamie had not even started the test.

Mr. Claxton took Jamie's test away. He wrote something down on it. He gave the test back to Jamie.

He had drawn shark teeth on some of the greater-than and less-than signs. Jamie frowned.

"Do you want to take a break?" Mr. Claxton asked.

Jamie shook his head. When it was time to hand the test in, Jamie wasn't finished. He handed his test in upside down, so nobody would see it.

Mr. Claxton looked at Jamie's test. Then he looked at Jamie and scratched his head. "Class, let's go to the library," he said.

Everyone was excited. Everyone but Jamie.

The class lined up and walked to the library. Jamie liked to run his fingers along the walls in the hall. But Mr. Claxton always told Jamie to keep his hands to himself. Today Jamie dug his hands into his pockets.

At the library, Jamie usually rushed to the shark books. That's where he held his Shark Club meetings, even if he was the only member.

But today, Jamie sat on one of the chairs. He stared at the books on the shelves. He didn't want to take any out. All he could think about was Jaws.

On the way back from the library, the class stopped at the water fountain.

Jamie's tummy was so tight, he didn't want a drink. But his mouth was dry. He bent down and slurped back some water. He stood up and felt his tummy spin. "BUUUUUURP!"

"Eww," Eva said.

Miles stopped. He sniffed the air. "I smell something," he said.

"You smell Jamie's burp," Eva said.

"I know that smell," Miles said. "It's fish."

Jamie froze. "Uh, I had a tuna sandwich for lunch."

Miles shook his head. "No, I mean fish food. I have fish at home. Your burp smells like fish food."

Jamie stepped back. Everyone was looking at him. Even Mr. Claxton.

Jamie's eyes began to water. "All right, all right. I did it!" he screamed. "I ATE JAWS!"

The hall was silent.

"That's gross," said Eva.

"That's *awesome*," Miles and Kamal said.

The hallway filled with giggles.

Jamie felt helpless. He ran into the classroom and slammed the door behind him.

Jamie hid under Mr. Claxton's desk. Behind him, he heard the classroom door open and Mr. Claxton's heavy footsteps. "Jamie," Mr. Claxton said. "Come here, please."

Jamie crawled out from under the desk. He was in so much trouble. His parents would never let him have a pet. Mr. Claxton would be angry with him for the rest of the year.

"Jamie, look at me, please."

Jamie looked up. He was expecting Mr. Claxton to be angry, but Mr. Claxton was calm.

"Thank you for telling the truth about Jaws. Now, why did you eat him?"

Jamie told Mr. Claxton everything that had happened at lunch.

Mr. Claxton scratched his head. "Hmmm," he said.

Chapter Nine

Jamie was quiet for the rest of the afternoon. Everyone was giving him weird looks. People were whispering. This was the worst day EVER!

He walked home by himself. He felt terrible. Thanks to him, his class didn't have a class pet anymore.

When he got home, Jamie went into his room. He opened his piggy bank. There were lots of coins inside. He went downstairs and counted his money on the kitchen table.

"Why are you counting your money?" asked his mom.

"Because I have an idea. Can you please take me to the mall?"

Jamie's mom made a face. "You want to go to the mall?"

Jamie nodded.

On the way to the mall, Jamie was so excited, he tapped his fingers on the car window. He rocked his legs back and forth. Finally, they arrived.

"So, why are we here?" Jamie's mom asked.

"It's a surprise." Jamie walked past the toy store. He walked past the food court and stopped outside the pet store.

His mom stared at him. "Jamie, what are we doing here?"

"I had an accident today. I ate a betta fish."

Jamie's mom nodded. "Yes, I heard about that from Mr. Claxton."

Jamie stepped inside the pet store. He walked past the puppies, the kittens and the hamsters. He even walked past the fish tanks.

Jamie stopped and pointed.

His mom's eyes widened when she saw what Jamie was pointing at. "That's an unusual pet," she said.

Jamie grinned. "I promise I won't eat it."

Chapter Ten

Jamie's mom drove him to school early the next day. He wanted to be the first to arrive.

Mr. Claxton was pleased to see the new pet. "I think everybody is going to be surprised," he said. "It is a very cool class pet."

He gave Jamie two cloths. One to cover the tank that held the new pet. And one to cover the small plastic box with holes at the top that Jamie had also brought.

When the bell rang, Mr. Claxton's class came inside and gathered on the carpet for circle time.

Jamie was so excited he could not sit still.

"Jamie, why were you here so early?" Kamal asked.

Jamie pointed to the covered tanks behind him.

"Oh, great," Eva said. "Let me guess. It's a shark."

Jamie shook his head. "I'm taking a break from sharks for a while."

"Jamie not talk about sharks?" Eva said. "I'll believe it when I hear it."

Kamal wrinkled his eyebrows. "Why are there two tanks? Did you get two pets, to make up for eating the last one?"

Jamie shook his head. "One tank is for our new pet."

"What's in the other one?" Eva asked.

"Come take a look," Jamie said.

Eva stood up and pulled the cloth away. "Gross!" she screeched. "It's full of bugs. Ewww!"

"Pet bugs?" asked Kamal.

"Those are crickets. They are not pets. They are food," said Jamie.

Miles groaned. "You are not going to eat crickets, are you?"

Jamie laughed. "The crickets are the food for our class pet." He pulled away the cloth on the other tank.

"Wow!" said Miles.

Everyone pushed toward the tank to look inside.

"What is it?" asked Eva.

"It's so weird," said Miles.

Jamie stood in front of the tank. "This is our new class pet. It's a gecko. A lizard."

The gecko was small enough to fit in someone's hand. It sat curled in an S shape. It was white with lots of black spots, like a leopard. The gecko looked at Eva and licked its yellow eye.

"Neat," Kamal said.

"At least he's colorful," Eva said, "even if he does look weird. Can we call him Rainbow?"

Everyone in the class seemed to like the name.

"Sure," Jamie said. "That's a great name, Eva."

Jamie smiled. Lizards were pretty cool. He had already started to teach himself about lizards.

The biggest lizard in the world was the Komodo dragon. One bite from it and you were a goner.

Jamie thought lizards were amazing. There were all sorts of things to learn about lizards.

Maybe he could start a lizard club!

Jeff Szpirglas and Danielle Saint-Onge live in Toronto and teach in classrooms with students of diverse cultural backgrounds. Jeff has written several books, including *Gross Universe* and *Fear This Book*, as well as scripts for radio and television. Before teaching, he worked at CTV and as the kids' page editor at *Chirp*, *chickaDEE* and *OWL* magazines. Jeff likes to play soccer, listen to heavy-metal music and make Danielle watch scary movies with him.

Danielle has a Master's degree in Social Anthropology and is an advocate for equity and social justice in the classroom. She has led summer workshops for new teachers and enjoys cooking and gardening. Whenever Jeff makes her watch a scary movie, she usually makes Jeff watch one about people in love.